James Marshall's Mother Goose

James Marshall's

# MOTHER GOOSE

SQUARE
FISH

Farrar, Straus and Giroux
NEW YORK

SQUARE
FISH

An Imprint of Macmillan

JAMES MARSHALL'S MOTHER GOOSE. Copyright © 1979 by James Marshall.
All rights reserved. Printed in March 2011 in China by
Macmillan Production Asia Ltd., Kwun Tong, Kowloon, Hong Kong.
For information, address Square Fish, 175 Fifth Avenue, New York, NY 10010.

Square Fish and the Square Fish logo are trademarks of Macmillan and
are used by Farrar, Straus and Giroux under license from Macmillan.

Library of Congress catalog card number: 79-2574
ISBN 978-0-312-58142-8

Originally published in the United States by Farrar, Straus and Giroux
Square Fish logo designed by Filomena Tuosto
First Square Fish Edition: September 2009
10 9 8 7 6 5 4 3
mackids.com

AR: 4.1 / LEXILE: NP

For my mother

Here we go round the mulberry bush,
The mulberry bush, the mulberry bush,
Here we go round the mulberry bush,
On a cold and frosty morning!

When pussy cat
Has got the gout,
The rats and mice
Can play about.

Hickory, dickory, dock,
The mouse ran up the clock.
The clock struck one,
The mouse ran down,
Hickory, dickory, dock.

Peter, Peter, pumpkin eater,
Had a wife and couldn't keep her;
He put her in a pumpkin shell
And there he kept her very well.

Little Boy Blue, come blow your horn,
The sheep's in the meadow, the cow's in the corn!
But where is the boy who looks after the sheep?
He's under the haystack fast asleep.

Elsie Marley has grown so fine,
She won't get up to serve the swine,
But lies in bed till eight or nine.
Lazy Elsie Marley.

Pease porridge hot,
Pease porridge cold,
Pease porridge in the pot
Nine days old.

Little Poll Parrot
Sat in her garret,
Eating toast and tay;
A little brown mouse
Jumped into the house,
And stole it all away.

Little Tommy Tittlemouse
Lived in a little house;
He caught fishes
In other men's ditches.

Betty Botter bought some butter,
But, she said, the butter's bitter;
If I put it in my batter
It will make my batter bitter,
But a bit of better butter
Will make my batter better.
So she bought a bit of butter
Better than her bitter butter,
And she put it in her batter
And the batter was not bitter.
So 'twas better Betty Botter
Bought a bit of better butter.

I had a little hen,
The prettiest ever seen

She washed up the dishes
And kept the house clean

She went to the mill
To fetch me some flour

And always got home
In less than an hour

She baked me my bread,
She brewed me my ale

She sat by the fire
And told a fine tale.

Barber, barber, shave a pig.
How many hairs to make a wig?
Four and twenty, that's enough.
Give the barber a pinch of snuff.

There was a rat, for want of stairs,
Went down a rope to say his prayers.

If chickens roll in the sand,
A rainy day is at hand.

Rain, rain, go away,
Come again some other day.

Humpty Dumpty
Sat on a wall

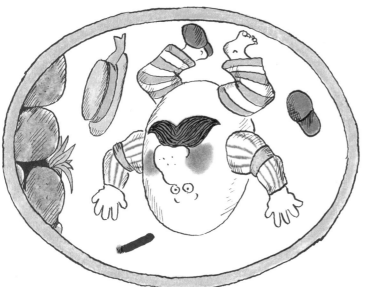

Humpty Dumpty
Had a great fall

All the King's horses
And all the King's men
Couldn't put Humpty
Together again.

There was a little girl,
And she had a little curl
Right in the middle
Of her forehead

When she was good,
She was very, very good

But when she was bad,
She was horrid.

I am Queen Anne, of whom 'tis said
I'm chiefly famed for being dead.
Queen Anne, Queen Anne, she sits in the sun,
As fair as a lily, as brown as a bun.

This little pig went to market

This little pig stayed home

This little pig had roast beef

This little pig had none

And this little pig cried wee-wee-wee-wee all the way home.

One, two, three, four, five,
Once I caught a fish alive,
Six, seven, eight, nine, ten,
Then I let it go again.

Swan swam over the sea,
Swim, swan, swim!
Swan swam back again,
Well swum, swan!

She sells seashells on the seashore;
The shells that she sells are seashells, I'm sure.
So if she sells seashells on the seashore,
It's seashore shells she sells for sure.

There once were two cats of Kilkenny,
Each thought there was one cat too many.

So they fought and they fit,
And they scratched and they bit,
Till, excepting their nails
And the tips of their tails,
Instead of two cats, there weren't any.

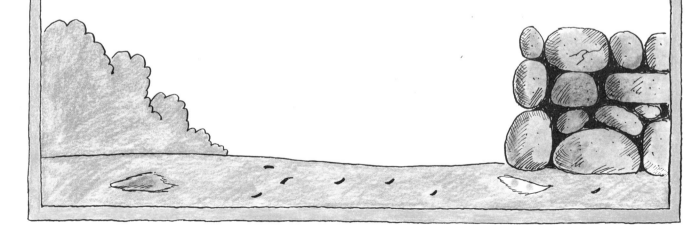

To market, to market, to buy a fat pig,
Home again, home again, jiggety-jig.

To market, to market, to buy a fat hog,
Home again, home again, jiggety-jog.

Solomon Grundy,
Born on a Monday

Christened on Tuesday

Married on Wednesday

Took ill on Thursday

**Worse on Friday**

**Died on Saturday**

**Buried on Sunday**

**This is the end
Of Solomon Grundy.**

Jack Sprat could eat no fat,
His wife could eat no lean,
And so betwixt them both, you see,
They licked the platter clean.

Old Mother Hubbard
Went to the cupboard,
To fetch her poor dog a bone;
But when she got there
The cupboard was bare
And so the poor dog had none.

Three young rats with black felt hats

Three young ducks with white straw flats

Three young dogs with curling tails

Three young cats with demi-veils

Went out to walk with three young pigs in satin vests and sorrel wigs

But suddenly it chanced to rain and so they all went home again.

Oh, Mother,
I shall be married to
Mr. Punchinello,
To Mr. Punch,
To Mr. Joe,
To Mr. Nell,
To Mr. Lo.
Mr. Punch, Mr. Joe,
Mr. Nell, Mr. Lo,
To Mr. Punchinello.

Smiling girls, rosy boys,
Come and buy my little toys;
Monkeys made of gingerbread,
And sugar horses painted red.

Pussy cat, pussy cat, where have you been?
I've been to London to see the great Queen.
Pussy cat, pussy cat, what saw you there?
I saw a little mouse under the chair.

Old King Cole was a merry old soul,
And a merry old soul was he;
He called for his pipe, and he called for his bowl,
And he called for his fiddlers three.

Hey diddle diddle
The cat and the fiddle

The cow jumped over the moon

The little dog laughed
To see such sport

And the dish ran away
With the spoon.

Fal de ral daddle
A pig on a saddle

The cat jumped over the house

The dog with the fiddle
Cried hey diddle diddle

And the trap ran off
With the mouse.

Bow-wow, says the dog;
Mew-mew, says the cat;
Grunt-grunt, goes the hog;
And squeak goes the rat.

Tu-whu, says the owl;
Caw-caw, says the crow;
Quack-quack, says the duck;
And what sparrows say you know.

So, with sparrows, and owls,
With rats, and with dogs,
With ducks, and with crows,
With cats, and with hogs,

A fine song I have made,
To please you, my dear;
And if it's well sung,
'Twill be charming to hear.